Fred Van Lente Writer
Rafa Sandoval Penciler
Roger Bonet Inker
Martegod Gracia Colorist
Dave Sharpe Letterer
Skottie Young Cover
Irene Lee Production
Nathan Cosby Asst. Editor
Mark Paniccia Editor
Joe Quesada Editor in Chief
Dan Buckley Publisher
Spotlight
MARVEL®

VISIT US AT
www.abdopublishing.com

Reinforced library bound edition published in 2009 by Spotlight, a division of the ABDO Group, 8000 West 78th Street, Edina, Minnesota 55439. Spotlight produces high-quality reinforced library bound editions for schools and libraries. Published by agreement with Marvel Characters, Inc.

Library of Congress Cataloging-in-Publication Data

Van Lente, Fred.
Pirated! / Fred Van Lente, writer ; Rafa Sandoval, penciler ; Roger Bonet, inker ; Martegod Gracia, colorist ; Dave Sharpe, letterer ; Skottie Young, cover. -- Reinforced library bound ed.
p. cm. -- (Iron Man)
"Marvel."
ISBN 978-1-59961-591-2
1. Graphic novels. [1. Graphic novels. 2. Superheroes--Fiction.] I. Sandoval, Rafa, ill. II. Title.
PZ7.7.V26Pi 2009
[Fic]--dc22

2008033397

Spotlight

All Spotlight books have reinforced library bindings and are manufactured in the United States of America.

HE BERMUDA TRIANGLE:
EDIMENT
ELOCITY:
IGH
ELECTRICAL
RESISTIVITY:
LOW
CHANCE OF
LOCATING GAS
HYDRATE: 0%
Another
dead end...

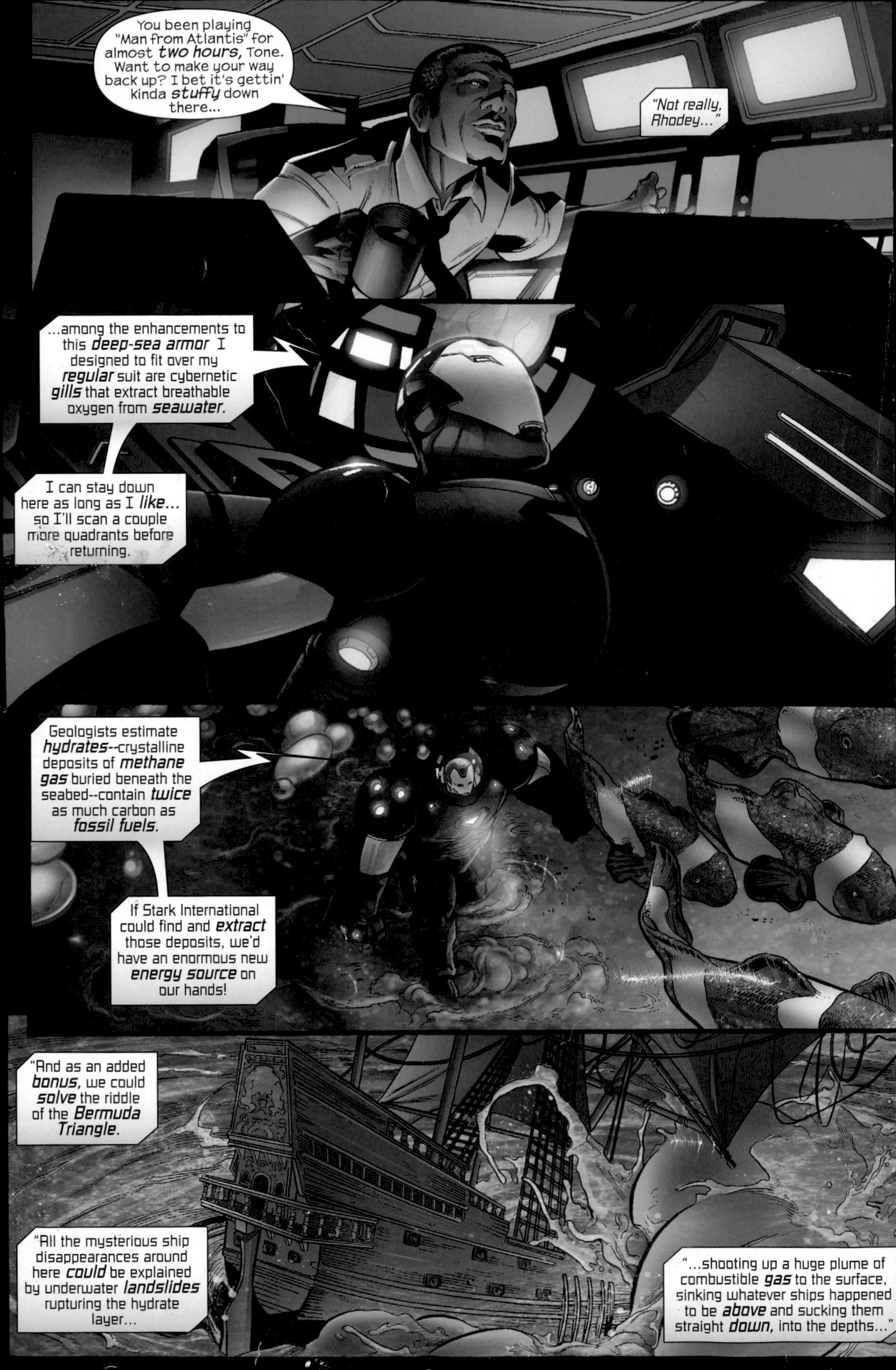
You been playing "Man from Atlantis" for almost two hours, Tone. Want to make your way back up? I bet it's gettin' kinda stuffy down there...
"Not really, Rhodey..."
...among the enhancements to this deep-sea armor I designed to fit over my regular suit are cybernetic gills that extract breathable oxygen from seawater.
I can stay down here as long as I like... so I'll scan a couple more quadrants before returning.
Geologists estimate hydrates--crystalline deposits of methane gas buried beneath the seabed--contain twice as much carbon as fossil fuels.
If Stark International could find and extract those deposits, we'd have an enormous new energy source on our hands!
"And as an added bonus, we could solve the riddle of the Bermuda Triangle.
"All the mysterious ship disappearances around here could be explained by underwater landslides rupturing the hydrate layer...
"...shooting up a huge plume of combustible gas to the surface, sinking whatever ships happened to be above and sucking them straight down, into the depths..."

Whoa.
Just like *that.*
The theory goes that ships would get dragged down so *quickly* by the methane blowout, they would be completely *buried* underneath tons of settling sediment...
... so I know hydrates weren't responsible for *this* shipwreck.
But it's quite a *sight* all the *same.*

Wha...?
And you brought friends.
DEFENSE MODE: ACTIVATED
I may be a lot slower down here with thousands of pounds of water pressure bearing down on me...
KKKRRRZZZZZZZZZZZ
...but I'm far from defenseless!
FWOOSH!
FWOOSH!
FWOOSH!
FWOOSH!
MINI-TORPEDO TARGETS: ACQUIRED
BOMF! BOMF!

Ask a stupid question...
Rhodey-- Rhodey, *come in.*
Sorry I missed the "No Trespassing" sign...
...which I don't think is even *legal*, out here in *international waters...*
...but what *exactly* were you trying so hard to *protect*--
RRRRUUUMMMBBBLLE
Rhodey, I need you to contact naval thorities *immediately*. I've stumbled upon--
ARNING: GNAL AMMED
NNECTION: AILED
Boot Water Impellers: FULL SPEED
I'm on my *own*...

WHIRRRRRRRRRRRR
Too slow!
This suit's so much bulkier and more unwieldy than my regular armor...
Well, ain't this an exotic catch o' the day, me mateys! A diving bell with legs!
A wee on the minnow side, though-- I'm of half a mind to throw 'im back!
I'd better start hearing where I am and who you are, or I start punching hole in your squidmobile--
Now he's gone and flown his true colors--a landlubber barely standin' on his sea legs!
Who else would spout off when the Captain's speakin'?

Shut your bilge-hole! I'll keelhaul you just as soon as look at you!
COMMANDER KRAKEN broaches no mutiny on his ship!
Unnnnnhh...
CLACK!
CLACK!
CLACK!
BEEP!
Don't damage him too badly, Cap'n, there might be some first-rate salvage in that shell!
You're as sharp as a cutlass, Jack Tar, don't let any man above or below water tell you otherwise!
All right, mateys, strip the fish clean, starting...
CLICK!
...now!
Seems like that energy blast shorted out my defense systems...

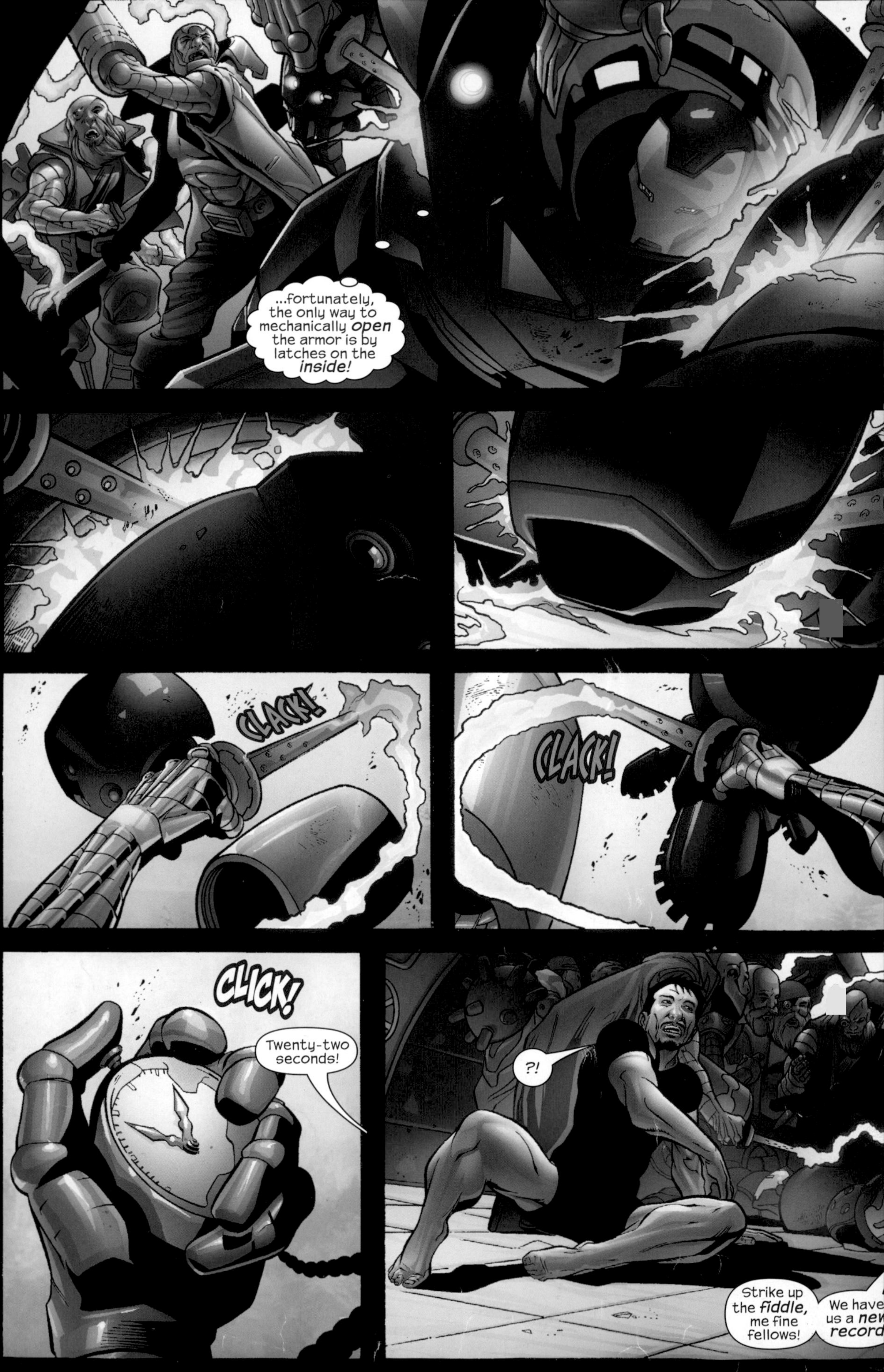
...fortunately, the only way to mechanically *open* the armor is by latches on the *inside!*
CLACK!
CLACK!
CLICK!
Twenty-two seconds!
?!
Strike up the *fiddle,* me fine fellows!
We have us a *new record*

Quite a haul, Cap'n! Magnetic esonance imagers n the eyes...mini-torpedoes in the shoulders...a Uni-Beam in the chest...
...might be just what we need to storm Hydrobase herself!
At last!
Hydrobase? The platform where they test all the experimental marine technology?
But that place is a floating fortress--oww!
KRAK!
Aye...hauled me before the mast... accused me of pilferin' me own inventions... I ask ye, how can I steal what's rightfully mine?
Like this sub I designed--and sailed away in, right under their own noses, and been the terror of the Caribbean ever since!
Don't you think the Cap'n knows that? He was their top scientist--before they threw 'im overboard!
But I swore I'd see those backstabbin' scientists walk the plank...
...and now, with these weapons and equipment, I got my chance!
Greeeeat... you really outsmarted yourself this time, Stark.
I plotted recent ship disappearances throughout the Bermuda Triangle, hoping to locate hydrate deposits that way...
...without ever realizing the real explanation was a band of 21st-century techno-pirates!
Cap'n! Off the starboard bow! A container ship!
Flyin' Singapore colors!
On-screen, Mr. 'Scope!

Aahh...a fine sight--practically keelin' over with consumer electronics!
Jam her radio, just as we did with our big metal guppy, here, so she can't send out a Mayday!
Battle stations! All hands on deck! No harm in fattenin' our hold en route to Hydrobase, eh, mateys?
As for you, my mustachioed dandy... why, you ain't even good for ballast. I'm afraid it's into the drink with ye...
...outta our torpedo tubes! Hahahahah!
Sorry, pal. Nothing personal. Captain's orders.
It doesn't bother you that your captain is clearly a raving lunatic?
A little--but you got to understand, we're all smugglers and castaways the Captain rescued at sea!
He saved our lives with cybernetics--we owe him everything! We can't betray him.
So he's obsessed with pirates. So what? Who doesn't like pirates?
Their victims, for one.
Well, you got us there.
CLANG!

Target within range!
FIRE TORPEDOES!
CHOOM!
CHOOM!

GASP!
Missed!
And the force of my ascent loosened my bonds.
Maybe my luck's starting to change...
BOOM!
BOOM!
BOOM!
Or not.

73 MINUTES LATER...
Unnh!! Pain in my joints has started...just as I feared.
De-compression sickness... "the bends" are setting in!
Because I surfaced so rapidly...my blood-stream is filling with nitrogen bubbles... Unnnh!
Doubly threatening to somebody with a heart condition like mine!
If I don't get treatment within a few hours...I'm through!
Can't call Rhodey--he'd never get here in time!
Let's see...the pirates stole the high-tech cargo, but I just hope...
Yes! They didn't bother with the electronics here on the bridge! The equipment's still intact!
In minutes I can jury-rig the ship's radio to track the transponder frequency continuously emitted by my armor components.
The crew didn't take every lifeboat when they abandoned ship...and she has an outboard motor. Good.
I've got to get my deep-sea armor back from Kraken!
Recompressing in its open-oxygen resuscitator is my only hope!

HYDROBASE:
This thing is giving me a headache.
Aye, I'd wager the cranial interface is set to the regular user's brainwave patterns--so your gray matter's gettin' bioelectric feedback.
Tell me quick, then--with the magnetic image resonator--am I any closer to blasting through the lock mechanism?
Almost...
"...maybe two or three more inches.
"And knock off the Long John Silver talk, huh?
"It's not like the Captain's in earshot."

Oh. Heh. Yeah... sorry.
Cooped up in that sub for weeks at a time...
...I sometimes forget how to sound like a normal person.
KLONGG!
Lucky those two went down quick...so dizzy, I can barely see... my spine feels like it's trying to climb out of my back...
NITROGEN NARCOSIS TREATMENT PROGRAM: RUNNING
Just pray... I made it in time...
PURE OXYGEN: RELEASED
Wheeeeze...
That was close...even by my standards.
Now I've got to track down the rest of the armor...

"...before these pirates cause any *permanent* damage with it."
Make yourselves *comfy*, eggheads!
KKKKRRRRZZZZZZ
I'm turning this *closet* into the Hydro-base *brig!*
No... *dead!*
Hunk of *junk...*
Watch your *mouth*.
The helmet can emit a remote *override signal* to *any* individual armor component.
Still, *your* gut's got no protection against my *cat-o'-nine-tails--*
SNAP!
I like my odds.
Wait! He's up-stairs--at the *highest* point of the base...

"...keeping his promise!"
N-now let's not be so hasty, Steve...
M-maybe we can talk to the authorities...get that embezzlement indictment dropped...
The one you call "Steve" is no more! You made sure o' that!
Now you're beggin' for your lives from Commander Kraken, scourge of the seven seas...
...and he ain't known for his mercy!
Kraken! Stop!
Why, if it ain't the Human Torpedo!
Maybe you got more o' the old salt in you than I thought...
THOOM
...but you still got the speed of a beached whale!
THOOM!
SHRAKKK!

AAAAAAAAA!
Good news: I've *got* you!
Bad news: I didn't bother to put *airborne jets* into my deep-sea armor!
Falling this *high up* into water is as bad as falling to the *ground!* We'll hit the ocean like it was *concrete!*
Not necessarily...

Floatation Devices: DEPLOYED
BWOMPF!
SPLASH!
Quickly, get up there, before Kraken gets back to his sub--
Geez, this suit is slow.
I'll not forgive your foiling my vengeance, landlubber!
As Ahab cursed the White Whale--
Full speed ahead, mateys! I won't rest until I've returned every shot he's fired across my bow in kind!

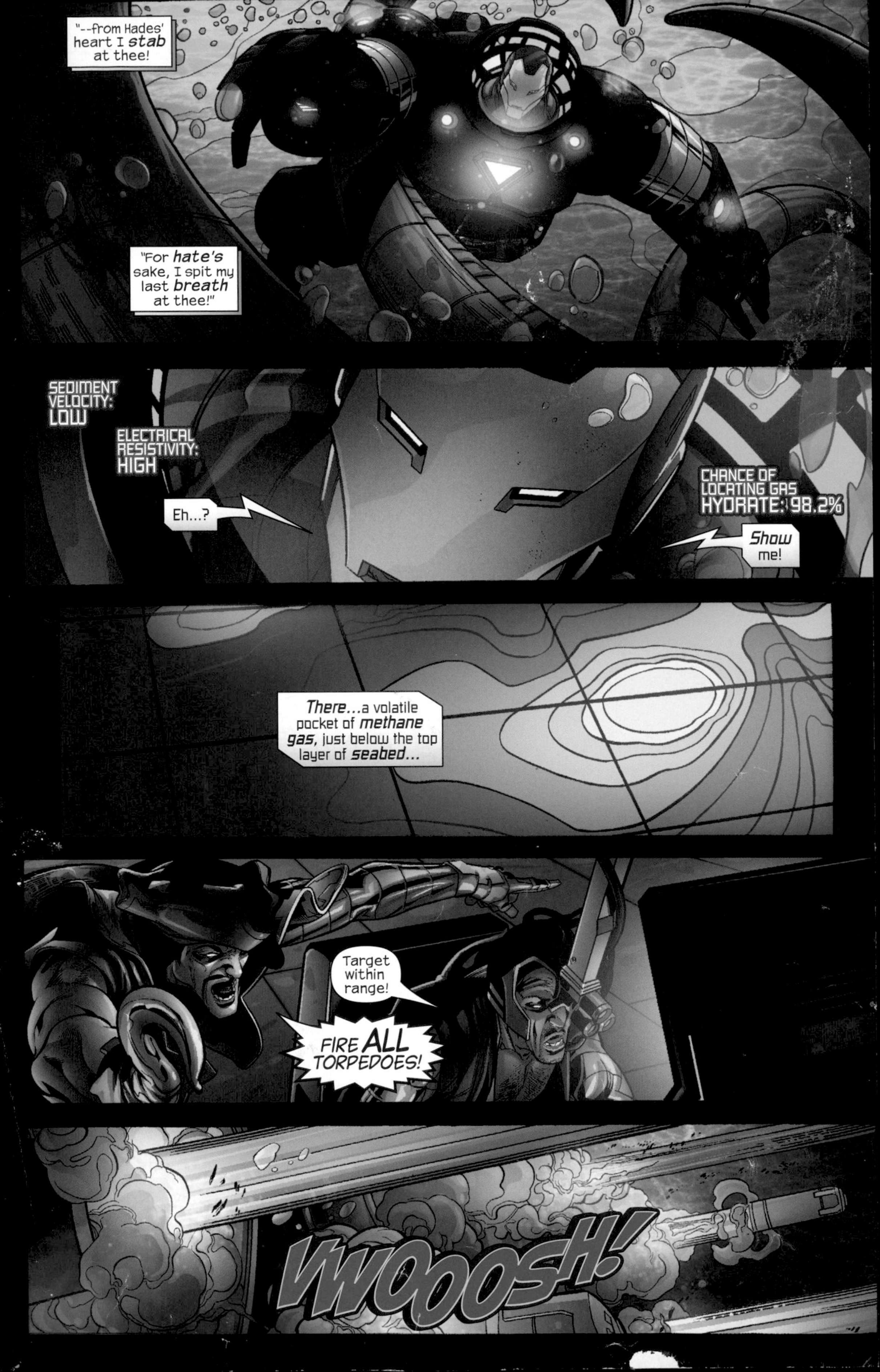
"--from Hades' heart I stab at thee!
"For hate's sake, I spit my last breath at thee!"
SEDIMENT VELOCITY: LOW
ELECTRICAL RESISTIVITY: HIGH
Eh...?
CHANCE OF LOCATING GAS HYDRATE: 98.2%
Show me!
There...a volatile pocket of methane gas, just below the top layer of seabed...
Target within range!
FIRE ALL TORPEDOES!
VWOOOSH!

Gotta dodge--*now!*
BOOM! BOOM! BOOM!
NO!!! We're bein' sucked straight down--
ROOGA! AROOGA! AROOG

HOURS LATER:
AREA SCAN: NEGATIVE
Incredible...I can't find a trace of Commander Kraken or his sub anywhere!
Like so many others, they've been swallowed up by the Bermuda Triangle!
THE END